This book belongs to:

SAMANTHA PELTZ

HAPPY 6th BIRTHDAY - YOUR PAL SCOTTIE

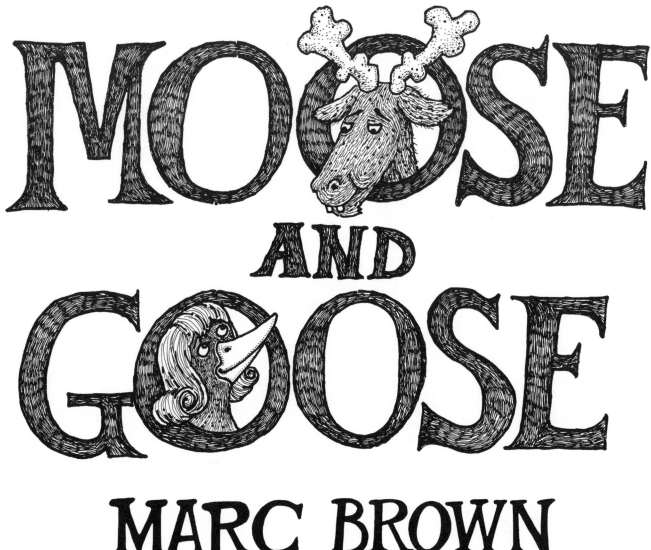

MOOSE AND GOOSE

MARC BROWN

A Unicorn Book • E. P. Dutton • New York

Library of Congress Cataloging in Publication Data

Brown, Marc Tolon.   Moose and goose.

(A Unicorn book)
SUMMARY: Two neighbors resolve their differences about noise.
[1. Noise—Fiction.   2. Friendship—Fiction.
3. Geese—Fiction.   4. Moose—Fiction]   I. Title.
PZ7.B81618Mo   1978   [E]   78-6822   ISBN 0-525-35175-2

Published in the United States by E. P. Dutton, a Division
of Sequoia-Elsevier Publishing Company, Inc., New York

Published simultaneously in Canada by Clarke,
Irwin & Company Limited, Toronto and Vancouver

Editor: Emilie McLeod
Designer: Riki Levinson
Printed in the U.S.A.   First Edition   10 9 8 7 6 5 4 3 2 1

for my Mother and Father

Moose was going to have a party.
He spent the morning cleaning. He practiced
his tap dancing while he ran the vacuum.

Goose was trying to take a nap.
Moose clattered down the stairs and banged on her door.

"May I borrow your piano?" asked Moose.
"Take it," said Goose.

She counted thirteen loud thumps
as Moose dragged the piano up the stairs,
then a tremendous crash!
"Moose, quiet!" said Goose.

Goose sat down to eat dinner.
There was a knock on the door.
It was Moose. "May I borrow your soap?"
"It's in the kitchen," said Goose.
Moose tapped his way up the stairs
to do his laundry.

He did the shuffle-ball change
as he sorted his socks.
Moose did his washing. Then he did his ironing.
Downstairs, Goose tried to enjoy her dinner.

"Moose, there's a flood down here!" screamed Goose.
Moose had left the water running.
The stairs had become a waterfall.
"Moose, the house is flooded!"
"Sorry. I'd help but my friends are here," said Moose.

Goose bailed and mopped
and watched Moose's friends arrive.
The first was the largest hippopotamus
Goose had ever seen. He was carrying a tuba.
Then came a bear with a drum.
The last guest was a baboon with a slide trombone.
"This is going to be some night,"
said Goose to herself.

When the last of the water was gone,
Goose was ready for bed.
"Maybe a warm cup of milk will help me sleep."
She had just finished her milk
when the music began. And it was loud!

Goose was desperate. She had to get
some sleep. She gathered every pillow
in the house and piled them on the bed.
Then she put a towel over her head,
placed a large vase over that,
and crawled beneath the pillows.

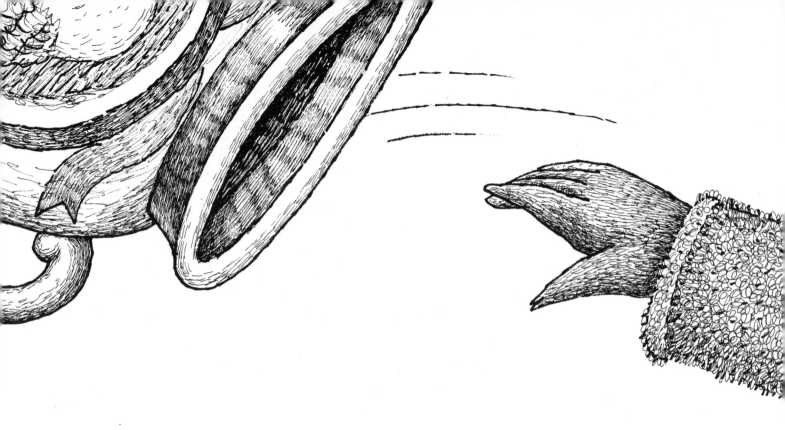

Under all that, Goose could still
hear the noise. The bed was shaking.
She was angry.
She threw off the pillows,
tore off the vase,
ripped off the towel,
and took out her earplugs.

"QUIET!" she screamed as she flew up the stairs.
"Quiet," she honked as she pushed in the door.
The music stopped.

"Moose, something has to be done! You've flooded
the house. You're always tapping above me.
You have the loudest parties in the world.
It's like living beneath a herd of elephants."
She honked and screeched.
Moose was speechless.
"Moose, you've got to move," said Goose.

"Why don't you switch apartments?"
said the hippopotamus. "Your piano
is already here."
"That's a great idea," said Moose.
"That's a lot of work," said Goose.
"We'll do the work," said Moose.
In no time at all, all of
Goose's things were upstairs.
All of Moose's things were downstairs.

Goose went to bed with only her earplugs.
She couldn't sleep.
Goose ran downstairs to see why it was so quiet.

Everyone was asleep.

"This has been some night,"
said Goose to herself.
She turned out the light,
snuggled beneath her quilt, and thought
how quiet it was above the treetops.
And the moon and stars
seemed so much closer.